Sunshine Superstars

Follow the Glitter Girls' latest adventures!
Collect the other fantastic books in the series:

And look out for:

Glitter Girls' Diary

Caroline Plaisted

Sunshine Superstars

■SCHOLASTIC

★ ♥ ★ ♥ ★ ♥ ★

Scholastic Children's Books,
Commonwealth House, 1-19 New Oxford Street,
London WC1A 1NU, UK
a division of Scholastic Ltd

London ~ New York ~ Toronto ~ Sydney ~ Auckland
Mexico City ~ New Delhi ~ Hong Kong

Published in the UK by Scholastic Ltd, 2003

Copyright © Caroline Plaisted, 2003

ISBN 0 439 97700 2

Typeset by Falcon Oast Graphic Art Ltd
Printed and bound by Nørhaven Paperback A/S, Denmark

2 4 6 8 10 9 7 5 3 1

★ ♥ ★ ♥ ★ ♥ ★

Chapter 1

It was Friday night and the Glitter Girls were making their way to the Energy Zone. Unfortunately, they weren't on their own – Meg's brother Jack and his best friend Nick were with them.

"You lot had better keep out of our way tonight," warned Jack.

"Yes," agreed Nick. "If we are going to beat you girls at the quiz, we'll need to keep our brains free from interference!"

"Interference?" exclaimed Zoe. "To your brains? I reckon they're too dense to have any room for interference!"

"Right!" laughed Flo.

"Well, we're here now," said Meg as they

arrived at the community hall. "So you won't have to wait long for us girls to trash you!"

"Oh, ha ha!" moaned Jack and Nick as they made their way inside.

"Hi, everyone," called Danny, the Energy Zone leader. "Sign in please and then we'll have ten minutes of free time before we start the quiz. That should give you time to get your brains in order."

"Hey, look – there's Ria!" said Hannah as she bounded off to the girls' zone.

Earlier in the year, the Glitter Girls had helped everyone at the Energy Zone organize a painting party to repaint the hall. Danny had given them the chance to make a boys' area and a girls' area. The girls had painted their zone in pink and purple and had decorated it with cool posters and lots of floor cushions – they all loved it.

"So have you all been reading the papers and watching the news to make sure your general knowledge is up to scratch?" Meg asked as she and her friends settled down on to the bean-bags and scatter cushions in their zone.

"Course," said Charly.

"We've got to win this quiz," said Hannah.

"Too right," said Zoe. "Those boys will go on and on about it if they win."

In fact it was the boys going on about being better than the girls that had given them the idea to do the quiz in the first place. At the last Energy Zone meeting, Danny'd declared that he was fed up with the constant rivalry, and told them to stop going on about it. But then Meg had said why not have a quiz and then they could prove if the boys were right or not once and for all. Everyone thought it was a great idea – including Danny, who had agreed to set questions about all sorts of topics: geography, television, sport, music, history. He'd even told them that he was going to do some mental maths!

"Right, you lot!" yelled Danny over the buzz

of noise from the Energy Zoners a short while later. "I think everyone's here. Can you all gather round? It's time for the quiz."

For once, the boys rushed to their seats.

"What's wrong with you girls?" asked Will as the girls made their way to their seats. "Scared you'll embarrass yourselves?"

"In your dreams, Will!" laughed Hannah, settling herself down next to her four best friends.

"OK," said Danny. "There are ten rounds with five questions in each round. As we haven't got the glory of modern technical gizmos, when the girls think they know the answer you call out 'SQUEAK!' Boys, you call out 'HONK!' You can confer with your team if you like. Got that?"

"Yes!" came shouts from both sides of the hall.

"Danny – can we just have a moment to talk tactics?" Meg asked.

"Oooooh! Get her!" said Fizz, who was one of Jack's friends.

"What's wrong? Scared?" giggled Jack.

Meg glared at her brother as she waited for the girls to huddle round.

"What is it?" Charly asked.

"I was just thinking," said Meg. "If someone absolutely knows the answer to something, that's fine. But if we're not sure of the answer I think we ought to confer like this, otherwise, if we talk openly in front of the boys they might hear our answer and use it before we do!"

"Of course!" agreed Flo, and the other girls nodded their agreement.

"Ready?" Zoe asked.

"Let's go," the girls nodded and settled back down in their seats.

"Boys, are you OK?" Danny asked.

"As always," said Jack with a smug look on his face.

"Girls?" Danny looked over at them. They nodded back.

"OK," Danny said, picking up his list of

questions. "The first round is about music. Question one: which singer or band stayed at number one for twelve weeks last year?"

The girls versus boys quiz had begun!

★ ♥ ★ ♥ ★ ♥ ★

"Which continent did Christopher Columbus discover?"

"HONK!"

"SQUEAK!"

The girls and boys were neck and neck in points and it was the last question in the last round of the quiz.

"OK," said Danny. "The boys just got there first."

"No!" wailed Meg. "It was us!"

"No it wasn't!" taunted Jack and Nick.

Unfortunately, they were right, the boys had answered first.

"Sorry Meg, boys first," said Danny.

"Noooooo!" moaned the girls.

"It was America!" said Nick smugly.

"Correct," said Danny.

And before he could say anything else, he was drowned out by the noise of the boys cheering their own victory. They had won by just one point!

"Boys rule! Boys rule!"

"Win-ners! Win-ners!"

"They are so childish," said Ria, crossing her arms in irritation.

"Pathetic," agreed Chenzira.

"Not listening!" said Zoe, putting her fingers in her ears and glaring at the boys.

"Calm down, everyone!" pleaded Danny. "Quiet please!"

He held his arm up in the air – the signal for everyone to fall silent and listen – and as usual, the girls got the hint first. It seemed to take ages for the boys to realize, but eventually the room fell silent.

"At last!" said Danny. "Now – well done to the

boys and commiserations to the girls. It was a close call."

There was a mixture of groaning and cheering around the room.

"That's enough, you lot!" Danny said. "Honestly, what a rabble. Now then, listen up. I've got some news to share."

"Ooooh," the Energy Zoners murmured and then the room fell silent as everyone listened expectantly.

"So," Danny continued. "We've only got six weeks to go before the summer holidays start and, as most of you know, we usually try to organize some kind of camping weekend."

There was a general roar of approval from around the room.

"Anyway, this year we've got the chance to do something different," Danny said. "Something a bit special. We've been offered some places at Camp Sunshine."

"Yeah!" came the general exclamation of

approval from around the room.

"Camp Sunshine!" said Jack. "Brilliant!"

"Cool," agreed Nick.

"Camp Sunshine?" said Charly to her best friends. "That's the place where you get to do all those great activities, isn't it?"

"Yes!" grinned Meg. "I saw it on the holiday programme. It was brilliant. They have all sorts of sports facilities and pony-trekking and stuff."

"So you all think it's a good idea, then?" said Danny, smiling at the Energy Zoners.

There was a cheer of agreement.

"OK," Danny continued. "There aren't enough places for everyone so it will be first come first served. And it's not that cheap either, I'm afraid."

"But when is it?" Nick asked.

"We'd be going as soon as the school holidays start," explained Danny. "You all remember my mate Joe who helped us paint the hall?"

The Energy Zoners certainly did. He'd been a really good laugh.

"Well, he's coming with us. It's for one week. I've got a letter and a leaflet for you all to take home with you. It explains all about it and how much it costs. Right – who's interested?"

A sea of hands went up around the hall.

"OK, take a letter and leaflet each and pass them on," Danny grinned. "I'll need to know by Monday if you want to come."

"It sounds great!" said Meg, as the Glitter Girls huddled together.

"We've got to go!" agreed Zoe.

"Do you think our parents will let us?" Hannah wondered.

"It depends how much it costs, doesn't it?" suggested Charly.

"Sounds like we need a meeting!" said Flo.

"Of course!" said Meg. "Tomorrow at my house, after lunch?"

"Go Glitter!" her best friends agreed.

Chapter 2

RAT-tat-tat!

There was a knock at Meg's bedroom door.

"Who's there?" she asked.

"GG!" came the whispered reply.

Meg opened her bedroom door and Charly, Flo, Zoe and Hannah hurried inside.

"Hey, love the mirror!" said Flo, touching the pink marabou that surrounded a new mirror next to Meg's wardrobe.

"It's so cool," agreed Hannah, settling herself down on the floor. "Where'd you get that?"

"Girl's Dream," explained Meg. "I bought it with the pocket money I'd saved up."

"So who's read the brochure about the holiday?" Zoe asked excitedly.

"Who hasn't?" said Charly, smiling.

"Camp Sunshine sounds fantastic, doesn't it?" grinned Flo.

"Too right," said Hannah. "They've got a great activity centre and one of those rope walks."

"There's a swimming pool too," added Zoe.

"And it's near to the beach!" exclaimed Charly.

"You get to sleep in these special six-berth cabins as well," said Meg.

"We've got to go!" urged Hannah.

"Danny's leaflet says that we'd leave on the Saturday after we break up from school," said Meg, reading as she talked. "No one's already going on holiday then, are they?"

"Not me," said Hannah.

"Nor me," said Charly and Flo at the same time.

"I might be going to stay at my gran's with my sisters some time during the holidays," said Zoe. "But we haven't decided when yet."

"So we could all go?" said Charly excitedly.

"If our parents say yes!" said Flo.

"But it costs quite a lot, doesn't it?" Zoe warned.

"Yes," said Meg. "But we've still got the money we earned from the Ice Brite ad campaign, haven't we?"

"Yes!" said Flo, pushing a stray piece of hair back behind her ear. "We could use that! Sorted."

"Not quite," muttered Hannah.

"What do you mean?" asked Zoe.

"Well, I haven't even asked my parents about the holiday yet," explained Hannah.

"I mentioned it," said Flo. "But I didn't realize how much it cost until now."

"My mum knows about it – Jack came home yesterday and blabbed about it straight away," said Meg.

"Did she say you could go?" Charly asked.

"She said she'd call my dad and ask him what he thought – she sounded quite keen on it, especially when I said I wanted to go too."

"So you think you'll be going?" wondered Zoe.

"Well, I hope so," said Meg. "But only if you lot are coming. I don't think I could bear being with Jack and Nick on my own. All that showing off."

"But if we all go," said Hannah with a wicked smile on her face, "we'd have a chance to teach those boys a thing or two, wouldn't we?"

"Girls against boys!" exclaimed Flo.

"With the girls winning!" laughed Charly. And all her friends giggled in agreement at the thought of proving that girls rule.

"If we say that we'll pay for the holiday ourselves from our Ice Brite money, then our parents will have to say yes!" said Hannah.

"Let's hope so!" said Charly, pushing her pink glasses back up on her nose with determination.

"Go Glitter!" her friends agreed.

★ ♥ ★ ♥ ★ ♥ ★

The Glitter Girls met up again on Sunday afternoon. This time, they were at Zoe's house and, because it was warm and sunny, they were making the most of the weather by having a picnic in the garden.

"You are so lucky you haven't got a stupid brother to pester you!" sighed Meg, settling down on the rug on the lawn. "If this was my garden, Jack would probably be water-bombing us from his bedroom window!"

The five girls groaned at the thought.

"Having big sisters is cool," agreed Zoe.

"Actually," said Hannah. "My kid brother isn't so bad."

"At the *moment*," warned Meg. "Wait until he gets a bit older!"

"He couldn't be as bad as Jack, could he?" sighed Hannah.

"He's a boy, isn't he?" said Charly. "Enough said!"

"So," said Meg. "Has anyone else spoken to their parents about Camp Sunshine?"

"Well, at first my mum kept on saying how expensive the holiday was and how I was already going on holiday with my family," said Charly. "But then I explained how we all wanted to pay for it with the money from our adverts and finally she said yes!"

"Great!" said Hannah. "So did my mum."

"My dad wasn't so sure about the outdoor pursuits," groaned Zoe. "He thought it sounded dangerous until he read in the leaflet about how everything is mega-supervised."

"So has he said you can go?" Meg asked.

"You bet!" Zoe grinned.

"Good," said Meg. "Because I can go too!"

"What about you Flo?" Hannah asked. "Please say you can come!"

"It wouldn't be the same without you!" agreed Charly.

"That's just what I told my dad," explained Flo. "That all the other Glitter Girls were going and that I'd be the only one who wasn't if he and mum said I couldn't go!"

"But you didn't know that we were all going last night!" exclaimed Hannah.

"I know." Flo grinned. "I told a bit of a fib . . . but it worked – they said yes!"

"Go Glitter!"

"So," said Meg. "Our parents have said we can go – which is great news. Now there's only one problem. . ."

"Problem?" asked Zoe. "What problem?"

"Danny said it was first come, first served, didn't he?" explained Charly.

"Oh. . ." sighed Hannah. "I see what you mean."

"So even if our parents have said yes, we still might not definitely be able to go!" Meg warned.

The girls muttered in agreement. Meg was

right. They'd just have to wait until Monday to find out whether they would get the chance to go on holiday together. . .

Chapter 3

It was an agonizing wait until the next meeting of the Energy Zone. In fact, the Glitter Girls were so desperate to go to Camp Sunshine that they persuaded their parents to ring Danny on Saturday to make sure he knew they wanted to go!

"Do you think our names are at the top of the list?" Charly whispered to the others as they settled down at the beginning of the meeting.

"Some of the others may have got their parents to speak to Danny on Saturday though!" warned Flo.

"Shhh!" hissed Meg. "Danny's about to speak."

"Hello, you lot," Danny greeted them.

"Hi Danny," everyone called back, and then they all fell silent.

"Some of you have already given me your Camp Sunshine forms – are there any more?" Danny asked.

A few hands went up – including Jack's, Nick's and the Glitter Girls'.

"Pass your forms round and I'll count them all up."

"Danny?" Meg said, putting her hand up. "You got the messages from our parents though, didn't you?"

"Yes, I did, Meg. But I've got to check the numbers," Danny explained. "I'll let you know how we're fixed at the end. Meantime, can everyone sign in please and then let's decide what we all want to do tonight."

The Glitter Girls groaned. The suspense was agonizing! But after the usual action-packed evening, Danny finally called everyone together again.

"OK," Danny said. "I've had a chance to check out the number of you interested in coming to Camp Sunshine."

"Please let him say we can go!" Hannah whispered, anxiously squeezing Zoe's and Meg's hands, who were sitting next to her.

"As it turns out," Danny continued. "We've still got two places left – if anyone wants them, let me know at the next meeting."

"Fantastic!" Meg grinned.

"We can go!" exclaimed Flo.

All the other Glitter Girls grinned excitedly.

The trip to Camp Sunshine was on!

At first the six weeks until the holiday seemed like a long time with only the usual routine and school to keep them busy. But as the weeks went by, the Glitter Girls got themselves organized and plotted and planned what they wanted to do when they got to Camp Sunshine and suddenly it didn't seem at all long until the end of term. Fortunately, the usual end of term excitement and fun stuff like Sports Day made the last days of school more interesting. Eventually, after packing and repacking, the week arrived, and the Glitter Girls were standing in the hall of Zoe's house early on the Saturday morning that they were leaving for camp.

"Looks like we're ready to go!" said Meg.

"Go Glitter!" said her friends in response.

Zoe's dad laughed. The rest of the Glitter Girls' parents had said their farewells and headed back to their own homes. Now Mr Baker was going to take the girls to the community hall so that they could meet Danny and get good seats on the coach. Jack had absolutely refused to arrive with the Glitter Girls and instead, Nick had slept over at Jack and Meg's house and they were going to the hall separately with Meg's mum.

"Come on," Mr Baker said, looking at his

watch. "We'd better get going or we'll be late. Can everyone carry their kit? Then we're off."

★ ♥ ★ ♥ ★ ♥ ★

It was a short drive from Zoe's house to the community hall.

"There's the coach!" exclaimed Flo as the car turned into the road leading to the hall.

"I hope we can all sit together," said Charly.

"Don't be daft," said Hannah. "The seats are in pairs, so one of us will have to be on our own, but hopefully Ria or one of the other girls can share."

"Yeah, or else one of us might have to sit with Jack," groaned Meg.

"No way!" said Zoe, pulling a face and making her friends giggle.

"Course we can sit together," said Charly. "If we bag the back seat then we can sit five in a row!"

"Good idea, Charly! Let's make sure we get on

first," grinned Zoe, determinedly. She said goodbye to her dad and the girls made their way over to where the Energy Zone members had congregated.

"Morning, girls," said Danny when he saw them a few seconds later.

"Hi Danny! Hi Joe!"

"Nice to see you again," smiled Joe. "You all ready for a great week then?"

"You bet!" confirmed Flo.

"Put your bags in the baggage compartment and then climb aboard please," Danny instructed, as he ticked the girls off his list. They got on board the coach and rushed towards the back.

"This is going to be brilliant!" sighed Hannah as she settled down into her seat.

"Uh-oh," tutted Charly, nodding towards the door of the coach. "Here comes trouble."

It was Jack and Nick.

"Go Glitter!" the two boys mocked, pretending to be the Glitter Girls.

"Oh, ha ha, Jack!" Meg said sarcastically.

"Sorry, the seats in front of us are taken," said Flo quickly, hoping that the boys wouldn't be complete pains and sit in front of them for the whole journey.

"Good – we wouldn't want to sit near you girls," Nick declared.

"Come on, you lot," warned Joe, who had boarded the bus to count everyone off against the list again. "Stop winding each other up and find somewhere to sit!"

"I am so excited," said Charly.

"It's just so cool to go away without our parents," agreed Hannah.

"For a whole week!" grinned Zoe.

"Go Glitter!" the others agreed.

It wasn't long before everyone was on board the coach and they were ready to go. The coach set off.

"Well, good morning to you all again!" said Danny from his seat near the driver. He was using a microphone so that everyone could hear him.

"Morning, Danny!" everyone yelled back, excitedly.

"Now that we're on our way, I thought I'd tell you about the added extra at Camp Sunshine this week," Danny said.

"What does he mean 'added extra'?" Hannah wondered aloud to her friends.

"I know how much you all enjoy team games, and the quiz we had a few weeks ago," Danny said.

"Certainly do," shouted Will. "Because the boys always win!"

"Oh, put a sock in it will you," called Govindi.

"Quieten down, everyone," said Danny. "Thank you," he continued. "Well, as I was saying . . . this added extra for Camp Sunshine – we have set a challenge for you. . ."

"What kind of challenge, Danny?" Charly asked.

"There'll be a different challenge every day," Danny explained. "And each team will have to win points."

"What kind of teams?" Fizz asked.

"Teams of five," Danny said. "It's up to you guys to decide on the teams. Then you give your team a name and let me know what it is."

The Glitter Girls looked at each other with relief and happiness. Teams of five meant they could all be together! And it was obvious what they'd call their team!

There was muttering all round the bus as everyone already started teaming up with their friends and chattering excitedly.

"As I've said," Danny continued. "You'll be given a challenge every day and you'll score points for how well you do in each challenge. By the end of the week, we should have one team that comes out as winner!"

"Yes!" said Zoe. "Now it's our chance to get even with the boys for winning the quiz!"

"What kind of challenges, Danny?" Jonny, one of Jack's friends, asked.

"Aah, that would be telling! Anyway, not knowing the challenges until they happen is another challenge!" said Danny.

"Ohh!" moaned the boys, slumping back into their seats.

"What's wrong, boys?" asked Ria. "Worried that you'll get beaten?"

"Worried that you girls will be no competition, more like!" Jack snorted.

"Sounds like loads of fun to me," Meg whispered to her friends. "Especially if we beat Jack and Nick's team."

"Go Glitter!" her friends agreed.

Chapter 4

A couple of hours later, the Energy Zone coach pulled into Camp Sunshine. Everyone looked around eagerly as the coach turned through some big gates and up a long drive. The Glitter Girls could see lots of gorgeous wooden houses which they guessed were the chalets they had read about in the leaflet.

"Hey, look at all those tennis courts!" exclaimed Zoe.

"And there's crazy golf too!" added Jack, quite forgetting in his excitement that he had said earlier that he didn't want anything to do with the Glitter Girls.

"There's a sign pointing to the swimming pool," Senami remarked excitedly.

There was so much going on at the camp, the Energy Zoners could hardly take it in. All around them they could see other buses and coaches bringing more children to the camp.

"Hey!" exclaimed Meg. "There's a girl standing over there with a sign that says 'Energy Zone'!"

And before they knew it, the Energy Zone coach had pulled up next to her. There was a boy standing there too.

"Hi!" the girl said, stepping on board the coach as soon as its doors opened. "I'm Becky and you must be the Energy Zoners – welcome to the best summer holiday you are ever going to have!"

There was a roar of approval from the bus.

"Come on, you lot," Joe said. "Grab your bags and let's get on with our holiday!"

★ ♥ ★ ♥ ★ ♥ ★

A short while later, the Energy Zoners were gathered together in a kind of common room.

They all hoped they'd have time to spend in there because there was a pool table, a karaoke machine, a huge television, and lots of games and books stacked on shelves.

At the other end of the common room was another group of children who looked a similar age to them. They'd arrived a bit before the Energy Zoners and were listening to another two adults wearing the same Camp Sunshine baseball caps and T-shirts as Becky and her companion.

The Glitter Girls looked at each other and smiled, just as Becky started to speak. "OK, welcome to Camp Sunshine. As I've already said, I'm Becky and I'm here to make sure you have a great holiday. I'd also like to introduce you to Dom. . ."

Becky gestured towards the boy who had been with her at the coach stop. He looked really cool and didn't seem much older than Zoe's sisters.

"Hi gang," Dom grinned. "If you need any-thing while you're here, just ask."

"OK," Becky explained. "You'll find a list of your cabins on the board over there –" she pointed – "and I'd suggest that you all find where you're sleeping and sort your stuff out first. How about we meet on the lawn outside in half an hour so that Dom and I can explain the rules of Camp Sunshine? Got that?"

"Got it!" everyone agreed.

There was a scramble as people grabbed their bags and raced towards the list of cabins.

"There's no way that Danny wouldn't have put us lot together, is there?" said Hannah.

"Doubt it," agreed Zoe.

It was Meg who got to the list first. "Yes!" she said, triumphantly.

"We're together?" asked Flo.

"Not just together," explained Meg. "We're on our own – just the five of us!"

"Go Glitter!"

"Come on – let's find our cabin," said Charly. "We're in number eight."

★ ♥ ★ ♥ ★ ♥ ★

"This is great!" said Zoe when they found their cabin.

And it was – like a perfect miniature house with its own veranda outside. Inside were three bunk beds and two small wardrobes with drawers underneath. In no time at all, the Glitter Girls had decided who was going to sleep where and unpacked their clothes.

"I love it here already and we've only just arrived," said Hannah.

"I wonder what our first challenge is going to be?" said Flo.

"Let's go back to see Becky and find out!" suggested Zoe.

"Go Glitter!" they all agreed.

Becky and Dom were talking with Danny and Joe when the Glitter Girls arrived at the lawn outside the common room. They were the first back.

"You're keen!" Becky smiled. "Ah – here come the others."

The other Energy Zoners arrived in dribs and drabs and sat around on the grass with the Glitter Girls, enjoying the warmth of the sunshine.

"Right, looks like we're all here, Becky," Danny said.

"OK – let's get started then," Becky said. "Is everyone happy with their cabins?"

"Yes," everyone agreed.

"Good. Any problems, let me know. You'll soon find your way around Camp Sunshine," Becky explained. "I think Danny and Joe have already explained that we've got a challenge-filled week of fun and adventure planned for you."

"Yes," added Dom. "We're going to start with our first challenge right now. . . First of all, have you all chosen your teams?"

"Yes!" the Energy Zoners replied enthusiastically.

"Good. You can tell us the team members and names before you begin your challenge, which is . . . orienteering," said Becky.

"Orienteering? Cool," said Nick.

"I haven't a clue what orienteering is," Zoe whispered to her friends.

"Don't worry," Becky grinned, sensing the group's concern. "Let me explain. In orienteering you are given a list of compass and map references. We're also going to give you some clues and the idea is that if you get everything right you should end up back here."

"And by following this challenge to get around Camp Sunshine, you'll soon get to know where everything is and feel at home!" Dom added.

"Great!" said Meg.

"OK?" Danny asked the Energy Zoners. "Come and tell us your teams, grab your map references and let's get orienteering!"

Chapter 5

Becky and Dom thought that the names the Energy Zoners had chosen for their teams were really cool. Jack's team had called themselves the Beastie Boyz which everyone agreed was highly appropriate. The other boys had grouped together to call themselves the Wild Wons. Senami and Ria and the other girls had decided to call their team the Animal Lovers. And, of course, no one from the Energy Zone was surprised to hear that there was a team called the Glitter Girls!

After the teams had been announced, Dom handed them all their map of the camp and their first map reference.

Because there were four different teams

taking part in the challenge, Becky had explained that each team was going to be given the same clues but in a slightly different order. That way she said they couldn't cheat by just trailing another team around the camp.

"So, what does it say?" Hannah asked as the Glitter Girls huddled around Charly, who was holding the map.

"It says 625750. And then there's a clue: 'my first is in sunshine but I'm all wet. You'll find me where lots of fun you'll get'," Meg read aloud.

"Well, we can work out the map reference from here," said Hannah. "It's like we did in school last term . . . here! That's where we've got to go!"

"What on earth does it mean?" wondered Charly.

"I haven't a clue," said Flo, laughing at her own joke.

"Look at that lot," Hannah sniggered, looking over her shoulder and seeing Jack's team, the

Beastie Boyz, laughing and messing around by the steps of the cafeteria.

"We've got to watch them because I don't trust them not to find a way to cheat. They'll do anything to win the challenge," said Meg.

"So come on, then," urged Charly. "How do we work out our first clue?"

"Yeah – what does 'my first is in sunshine' mean?" Zoe asked. "What's 'my first'?"

"I've done something like this before," said Hannah. "I think it's something to do with finding the first letter of the name of the place we're meant to be heading to."

"Hmm . . . sunshine. . ." said Flo, popping her thumb in her mouth, as she often did when she was thoughtful.

"What about this wet thing though – sunshine and wet at the same time don't seem to fit together. . ." Zoe pondered aloud.

"I think that's a trick," said Meg. "It's trying to confuse us. The letter we need is in the word sunshine but the place we are looking for where there's water. . ."

"Got it!" exclaimed Charly. "The shower block – it starts with S and it's a place that's wet! Let's check the map reference!" Charly began looking at the coordinates on the map.

"Nice one!" agreed Hannah. "Does it match the last bit of the clue, Meg?"

Meg read it aloud again. " 'You'll find me where lots of fun you'll get'."

"Oh, now I'm not so sure," sighed Charly, looking up from the map. "I mean, my mum goes bonkers if Lily splashes about in the shower at home."

"Come on, you lot!" urged Zoe. "Look – the Beastie Boyz have already set off. It looks like they've already worked out their first clue."

The Glitter Girls turned round to see the boys looking very smug as they set off in the opposite direction.

"Swimming pool!" hissed Flo.

"They're not going that way," Hannah pointed out. "That's over there."

"No!" grinned Flo. "The swimming pool is where we should be going. It's wet, starts with S and it's where we have lots of fun!"

"She's right!" said Charly. "The showers marked on this map are right next to the swimming pool and the map reference matches it exactly. Come on!"

The Glitter Girls raced quickly in the direction of the pool but when they got there, they were puzzled. They couldn't find the next clue. They searched frantically but it was difficult because other children were in the pool playing a game of water polo. Even the changing rooms were crowded. The Glitter Girls split up so they could search better.

"This is hopeless!" sighed Charly when they regrouped at the entrance to the pool.

"I give up," moaned Flo.

"You can't!" exclaimed Meg, determined as ever. "The clue's got to be here somewhere."

"Hey, it's here!" said Hannah triumphantly, pointing out a long tube of clear plastic, attached to the wall next to the sign that read, *Welcome to the swimming pool*. At the bottom of the tube, they could see a piece of paper with the word *Clue* written on it. The paper was inside a plastic bag that was attached to a cork.

"How are we meant to reach that?" asked Flo, trying unsuccessfully to grab the clue at the bottom of the tube. All of the Glitter Girls tried to reach it, but the tube was longer than any of their arms, and they couldn't tip it upside down because it was clipped to the wall.

"We could try hooking it with a stick," suggested Zoe, looking around for a twig or something.

The Glitter Girls searched around for a stick

but even after their best efforts, they still couldn't reach the clue.

"This is so frustrating!" wailed Hannah.

"If we're not careful we'll spend our whole time on this first clue," moaned Charly.

"I can't believe how dumb we all are!" Hannah suddenly yelled. "Quick, get some water out of the pool with something. Try one of those things!" she said, pointing to the collection of pool toys in a box nearby.

"Why do you want water?" asked Zoe.

"To make the cork float!" Hannah explained.

"Of course!" said Meg, racing with Flo to collect some water with one of the beakers from the box.

Just seconds later, the Glitter Girls had their next clue.

"Come on," said Charly. "We'd better hurry up or the Beasties might beat us back!"

The orienteering certainly was proving to be a real challenge. The Glitter Girls worked out that their next destination was the rope walk. But they had to climb a large oak tree to retrieve the clue, which, after a lot of puzzlement, led them to the archery range. Becky was right about the challenge helping them to find their way around, because by the time they ended up back at the common room, they'd been round the entire place.

"Well done, everyone!" Danny said, when the last team arrived back.

Amazingly, all four teams seemed to finish within a few minutes of each other. They all congregated round a table where drinks were being poured for all the Energy Zoners.

"So who won the challenge, Danny?" Nick said, after he'd gulped down about half a gallon of juice.

The Glitter Girls looked at each other – if everyone had come back at the same time, how would Danny work out which team had won?

"Actually," he said, "today's challenge was a draw."

"A draw?" Meg asked. "How can that be?"

"Everyone was so smart today that you all got the clues right," explained Joe.

"But the Animal Lovers got here first!" wailed Senami, looking defiantly at her friends.

"I know," said Becky. "But we never said it was a race. Anyway, don't worry – tomorrow's when the real competition starts!"

"So what are we doing then?" asked Will. "What's our challenge?"

"That would be telling," said Danny. "You'll find out at breakfast tomorrow."

The Energy Zoners moaned in protest.

"Meantime. . ." Danny continued, "you all have some free time until the barbecue at seven this evening. You can do whatever you want until then."

A cheer of approval went up.

"Let's go swimming!" suggested Charly to her four best friends.

"Go Glitter!" they all agreed.

Chapter 6

Like all the other Energy Zoners, the Glitter Girls loved Camp Sunshine. There was so much to do! After a great time at the pool, where there was a fantastic flume, a slide and huge inflatable toys to climb on, the Glitter Girls joined everyone for a brilliant barbecue to celebrate the first night of their holiday.

Then it was off to their cabin to settle down for the night. Zoe and Hannah were sharing a bunk bed by the window and Charly and Flo shared another by the door. Meg was sleeping on the top bunk of the other bed, which was along the far wall.

"I wish we could always sleep all together in a little house like this," said Charly as they were changing into their pyjamas.

"It would be great, wouldn't it?" agreed Zoe.

"We could have fun all the time then," said Hannah.

But any ideas the Glitter Girls had about staying up and talking all night disappeared – as soon as their heads hit the pillow the five friends went straight to sleep!

★ ♥ ★ ♥ ★ ♥ ★

Next morning, Charly, Zoe, Hannah, Flo and Meg were woken by a horrible blasting noise which was coming from just outside their window.

"What was that?" Hannah screamed, her heart beating fast with the shock.

Meg leapt down from her bunk in her pink stripy pyjamas. "I think it was something outside."

Flo was nearest to the door, and she'd already jumped out of bed and was opening the door.

"Gotcha!" someone yelled, squirting Flo in the face with a giant water pistol.

"Arghh!" Flo spluttered. "I'm soaked!"

Hannah leapt out of bed and rushed out of the door. "Who's there?" she shouted, looking around.

But whoever it was had made a very swift exit – she couldn't see anyone.

"Who'd want to do that?" Charly asked.

"I bet it was one of those boys!" declared Meg.

"I bet it was too," said Zoe. "Let's go and get them back right now!"

"No – hold on," said Meg. "There's plenty of time to get our own back on them – if it *was* them. Come on, let's go and have breakfast and get today's challenge first. We can make a plan and get our own back on the Beasties when they are least expecting it."

"Go Glitter!" said her friends in response.

★ ♥ ★ ♥ ★ ♥ ★

"Enjoy your shower this morning, girls?" Jack giggled when the Glitter Girls arrived in the dining room for their breakfast. All around him the Beasties dissolved in hysterics.

"Just ignore them," hissed Meg as they sat down at the opposite table.

"So it *was* them," said Flo. "Huh!" She'd had to hang her pyjamas on the washing line so that they'd dry out by the evening.

"OK, you lot, listen up!" Danny called out as the Energy Zoners were finishing their breakfast a short while later. "Now – news of today's challenge."

The room fell silent.

"Today we're off to the fair!" Danny declared and there was a loud cheer of approval.

"Where's the challenge in that then?" asked Fizz, one of the Beasties.

"Well," said Becky. "Your challenge is to see how many points you can score on the games at the fair."

"What games are there?" Meg asked.

"A shooting range, Hook the Duck, Splat the Rat and a Hoopla where the further away the target the greater the score," Joe explained.

"Cool!" said Will.

"Scary!" whispered Zoe to her friends. "Some of those games are really difficult."

"No time to lose, you lot," Danny said. "Go and clean your teeth, fetch your jackets and meet us back at the coach in twenty minutes."

★ ♥ ★ ♥ ★ ♥ ★

It didn't take too long to get to the fairground and what a fairground it was! It was huge – certainly the biggest the Glitter Girls had ever been to. And it was right by the seaside at the end of the pier. There was a scary-looking roller coaster at the far end.

"This place is great," said Nick. "Can we have a go on some rides?"

"There'll be time for that after the challenge," Dom said.

"Yes – but in the meantime I want all of you to stick together," warned Danny. "We can't afford to lose any of you."

"OK, follow me, guys," said Becky. "Let's play Hook the Duck!"

Everyone trooped off behind Becky. Jack was so confident that he could hook ducks easily that he volunteered to go first. But it proved harder than Jack had thought and that, combined with the fact that all the other Energy Zoners were watching his every move, meant that he only managed to hook three of his five ducks in the end. The other Beastie Boyz didn't do much better and their team scored a total of 13.

Then it was the turn of the other teams: the Animal Lovers got 12 and the Wild Wons 13. The Glitter Girls were the last team to go. Meg went first, but she got them off to a bad start.

"Disaster!" Meg wailed – at the end of her round she'd only managed to score one point. "I'm really sorry, girls," she excused herself to her friends.

"What's wrong, little sister?" Jack said unkindly. "Find it a bit tricky, eh?"

"Don't worry about it," Hannah said. "Just ignore him. I'll probably be useless too."

But fortunately, Hannah wasn't. She managed to hook all five of her ducks – no one else had managed that.

Flo went next, but, like Meg, she found it difficult. She just didn't seem to get the technique of the hook, although she did manage to hook her last two ducks eventually.

"We've only got eight so far!" Flo sighed. "Zoe and Charly – you've got to make sure we beat the boys!"

"I'll go next!" Charly offered. Luckily, she was as good as Hannah and also got all five ducks! "Now we're the same score as the boys already!" Charly said, handing the hook to Zoe. "Zoe – it's up to you!"

Zoe gulped. The thought of being responsible for putting the Glitter Girls in the lead made her very nervous and her hand shook so much that she missed her first four ducks.

"You've got to get the next one!" Meg urged. "Please, Zoe – you can do it!"

"Useless! Useless!" the Beastie Boyz started to chant, making Zoe even more nervous.

"That's enough, you lot!" Joe warned. "Be quiet!"

"Yes!" screeched Zoe as she managed to hook her last duck.

"14 points to the Glitter Girls!" Becky declared. "That puts the Glitter Girls in the lead after the first round of today's challenge!"

"Huh!" moaned the Beastie Boyz. "You won't be there for long."

"That's what you think," warned Meg.

"Go Glitter!" grinned the girls.

★ ♥ ★ ♥ ★ ♥ ★

The next game they played was Splat the Rat.
Each player had to take a turn and whack the
"rat" with a cricket bat as it came out of the
bottom of a drainpipe. The rat turned out to be
a beanbag.

Everyone had five turns at hitting the rat and
it was a riot of noise and excitement. After some
furious calculations, Joe told them the news: the
Beastie Boyz had evened the score and were
now neck and neck with the Glitter Girls.

"Yes, yes, yes!" yelled the Beasties.

"No. . ." sighed the Glitter Girls.

★ ♥ ★ ♥ ★ ♥ ★

Next was the Hoopla. Something the Beasties
were better at than any of the other teams. The
Glitter Girls and the Animal Lovers both scored ten
points each. The Wild Wons scored ten as well. But
the Beastie Boyz were way ahead with 13.

"We'll have to beat them in the target shooting," Meg said, determined that they would.

But they didn't! The Glitter Girls only drew – like all the other teams, they only managed five points.

"So what's the result, Danny?" asked Jack eagerly as soon as the final round of the morning's challenge was over.

"Hang on," said Danny, as he and Joe busily totted up the scores. "OK. . ." The Energy Zoners fell silent, waiting to hear the news. "Wild Wons – 32. Glitter Girls – 33. Animal Lovers – 31. And, the Beastie Boyz . . . 36!"

"No!" wailed Zoe.

"We win! We win!" screeched the Beasties, jumping up and down with glee.

"Disaster!" said Charly to her friends.

"We'll just have to make sure we win tomorrow then!" Flo said. And her friends nodded fiercely, determined as ever.

Chapter 7

The Glitter Girls put the disappointment of the first day's challenge behind them and enjoyed the rest of their time at the funfair. After a yummy fish and chip lunch, Becky had given all of them a bag of tokens to pay for the stalls and each team was allowed to go around the fair with one of the leaders. The Glitter Girls were really pleased when they were told Becky would be accompanying them.

They had a great time on the rides: they went into the Haunted House, down the Helter Skelter, laughed themselves silly in the Hall of Mirrors and even managed to win a teddy each when they went back to hook more ducks! Flo and Hannah bought some candy floss and managed to get really sticky! But eventually, Becky told them that it was time to go back to the coach and return to camp.

Just like the day before, the Energy Zoners were allowed to choose what they did with the rest of the time back at Camp Sunshine before supper. The Glitter Girls loved the freedom they had at camp because you could do whatever activities you wanted. One of the camp leaders, even if it wasn't Becky or Dom, was always on duty at every section of the camp to have a laugh or point out other fun things to do. And the Glitter Girls loved making friends with the other children who were at camp too. Everyone was having a really great time.

★ ❤ ★ ❤ ★ ❤ ★

After breakfast the next morning, Dom announced the day's challenge. They were going on the coach to a nearby stable.

"Yes!" exclaimed Zoe, who was an excellent rider.

"Revenge!" said Meg, who knew that Jack and Nick were hopeless at riding.

"Listen, when we get to the stables," Dom explained, "we'll do a shortish trek this morning followed by a picnic lunch, and then we'll round off our day with a mini gymkhana."

"That's so not fair!" protested the Beastie Boyz.

"That lot go riding!" exclaimed Jack, pointing towards his sister and the other Glitter Girls who were grinning with pleasure.

"Lighten up, boys!" Danny warned. "I'm sure you'll all do OK."

"This is one challenge that I think we'll definitely do well at!" Meg declared.

"Go Glitter!" her friends agreed.

To make things fair, the people at the stables made sure that each Energy Zoner was given a pony that suited their ability in the saddle. Which meant that the Beastie Boyz ended up with plump slow ponies that were safe and steady.

Jack and Nick obviously felt more confident when they realized. But Zoe, who was a very experienced rider, knew better.

"They may think they're OK now," she whispered to her friends as they trotted off. "But wait until they take part in the gymkhana," she giggled. "Our quicker ponies will be much more likely to win the races!"

"I hope so." Flo smiled. "I think we need to get even with them."

"Especially as we haven't had the chance to sort them out after they gave Flo that soaking the other morning," said Charly.

"I've had an idea about that!" hissed Hannah.

"What's that?" her friends whispered.

But Danny and Joe were just behind them.

"Come on, you girls," Joe said, laughing. "Get a move on!"

"I'll tell you later!" Hannah winked.

★ ♥ ★ ♥ ★ ♥ ★

They all set off for the morning's trek. The first part of the trek followed a winding path next to a river, overhung with trees. It was very pretty and everyone was quiet, watching the wildlife and scenery. They continued like that for some time – the Glitter Girls up at the front and enjoying the ride.

Zoe turned out to be right about the Beasties' ponies – they were so slow they could barely keep up sometimes.

"Ride 'em, cowboy!" Meg turned to laugh at her brother who looked a bit uncomfortable in the saddle, at the back of the line.

"I'll get you!" warned Jack. But everyone laughed when his pony immediately ground to a halt and refused to budge an inch further.

"Good job we're ready for lunch." Dom laughed as he dismounted from his pony and tied it up.

Everyone else did the same and made sure the ponies had plenty of water to drink. Then the Energy Zoners all settled down to their lunch. It was a gloriously warm and sunny day and they all sat in the shade of some trees. The Glitter Girls made sure they sat as far away from the Beastie Boyz as they could.

"So, what's this idea?" Meg asked Hannah as she munched on her sandwich.

"An apple pie bed," Hannah declared. "You know, when you fold over the sheets so that you can't get into it properly."

"Good idea," said Flo. "But I'm not sure that's bad enough for those boys after the soaking they gave me!"

"Well – let's fill their beds with stuff as well," suggested Charly.

"But when will we get the chance to do that?" Flo wondered.

"Easy," said Meg, with a grin on her face. "During free time, before supper – when the Beasties are out."

"Brilliant!" said Hannah. "But first we've got to beat the boys at the gymkhana this afternoon."

"Go Glitter!"

There were no incidents with reluctant ponies for the rest of the trek and it wasn't long before they arrived back at the stables.

The mini gymkhana was all set up and as soon as everyone was ready the competition got going. As the Beasties had predicted, the Glitter Girls were very confident in the obstacle races. Becky decided that the less experienced riders could have their ponies led by one of the others in their team to make it easier. But when they did an egg and spoon race, the Beasties dropped most of their eggs because they were so wobbly in their saddles. Though they did a bit better in the next race, when they had to collect things with a big hook and then drop them into a bucket.

It was the last event where the Glitter Girls' experience really showed. The stable girls had laid a course in a sand ring and the teams had to take it in turns to go over jumps and in-between obstacles and bales. They'd made allowances for the less experienced riders so that it was fair – the more experienced riders were given penalties and the Beasties were allowed to miss the jumps out altogether.

"Result!" shrieked a delighted Zoe as Charly, the last member of the Glitter Girls, managed to finish with a clear round.

"Oh *dear!*" grinned Meg as she watched her brother Jack struggle not to knock over the buckets and complete the round for the Beasties.

"Do you think we're in the lead?" Flo wanted to know as she watched Becky, Dom and Danny adding up the scores at the end.

"I really hope so," said Hannah.

"What are the scores, Danny?" Senami asked, as she and the rest of the Animal Lovers gathered round.

"Well," he declared. "Today's winners are the Glitter Girls with five points, followed by the Animal Lovers with four, the Wild Wons with three and the Beastie Boyz with two."

The Beastie Boyz groaned. "So who's in the lead overall?" Nick wanted to know.

"It's a draw," Joe declared. "The Glitter Girls and the Beastie Boyz both have 38 and the Animal Lovers and the Wild Wons both have 35."

"I thought we'd be in the lead!" sighed Hannah.

"Me too!" moaned Flo.

"Well, at least we're not behind them any

more," said Charly, hugging her friends.

"Come on," said Zoe. "Let's get back to Camp Sunshine and make some apple pies!"

★ ♥ ★ ♥ ★ ♥ ★

When they got back to camp it was ages before the coast was clear, but finally the Glitter Girls saw Jack and Nick and their mates leave their cabin and head off towards the rope walk. Charly and Zoe followed them to make sure they were well out of the way, and then they raced back to the cabin to tell the others that the coast was clear.

"Come on," said Meg. "Let's do it. Zoe, can you keep watch outside? The rest of us will go and wreck those beds!"

The Glitter Girls had no time to lose because they were terrified they'd be caught. They raced over towards the cabins and tried to act casual. Flo hung around outside the boys' cabin while the others slipped around the back and then popped up from behind a bush to slip, one at a time, through the door.

"Fold the sheet back like this," Hannah showed them once they were in the boys' cabin.

"Look at all the chocolate they've got stashed in here!" said Zoe, pulling piles of chocolate bars out from one of the boy's bags.

"Let's stuff that in their beds!" Charly giggled. "Quick, take off the wrappers so it will go all gooey in the heat!"

"Yuck!" Zoe groaned. "It already is because it's so hot in here!" She dropped the melting chocolate on to one of the beds.

"Make sure you put the duvets back so that they don't get suspicious," warned Meg. "And bring the wrappers too. Come on!"

But the Glitter Girls didn't have to worry, because the boys spent ages at the rope walk and didn't even come back to their cabins before supper.

All the way through the meal, the Glitter Girls

giggled to themselves at the thought of the fate that was going to meet the boys that night. Revenge would be theirs.

At bedtime, the Glitter Girls waited in their cabin in anticipation until eventually they heard all sorts of yelling and moaning from the boys' cabin.

"Gotcha!" giggled Meg.

"Go Glitter!" The girls agreed, trying hard to stop laughing.

Chapter 8

"Is this true, girls?" Danny asked angrily the next morning as he held up the ripped and mucky remains of a sheet.

The Glitter Girls had barely had a chance to get dressed before Danny and Joe had knocked on the door and told them that Jack and the other boys were blaming them for the apple pie beds.

"Course it is!" said Jack, who along with the other Beastie Boyz had followed Danny and Joe to the Glitter Girls' cabin.

"And they ruined all our chocolate too!" spluttered Nick. "It's melted all over the place! Look at my sheet!"

Nick held up a gooey mix of chocolate and

sheet and looked so upset about his secret stash of sweets that Hannah, Zoe and Flo couldn't help but laugh.

"You see!" exclaimed Jack. "It *was* them!"

Charly and Meg were struggling to keep back their own laughter and tried to make excuses for themselves.

"If you thought it was us, why didn't you come and ask last night, Jack?" Meg wanted to know.

"Because," said Danny answering for Jack, "when they came in to me last night, I couldn't see the point of the whole of the camp being disturbed because of some stupid feud between you boys and girls."

"So come on," Joe demanded. "Was it you?"

The Glitter Girls felt a bit embarrassed. Yesterday afternoon it had seemed like a good laugh, but now, looking at the state of the sheets and seeing Danny's cross face, they just felt stupid. They didn't know what to say to

Danny and Joe. After all, they couldn't lie to them but saying it was their fault made them feel like idiots.

"Well?" said Danny. "What have you got to say?"

"OK," sighed Meg. "It was us. Sorry, Danny. But we were just trying to get them back for soaking Flo with the water pistol the other morning!"

"Yes, sorry, Danny," the others said too.

"It was a pretty stupid and childish thing to do!" Danny scolded them. "I don't care what they did to you – I expected more from you! What's more, your behaviour reflects badly on the entire Energy Zone."

"Sorry. . ." the Glitter Girls said again.

"I'm afraid I can't let this go without some form of punishment, girls," Danny warned. "You lose two points from your score."

"But you can't do that!" protested Hannah.

"Sorry, girls," Joe explained. "I don't think you've left us with any choice."

"But that means that the boys are in the lead!" Zoe wailed.

"Ha ha!" sniggered Jack.

"Serves you right!" laughed Nick.

The Glitter Girls were left speechless as they realized that the Beastie Boyz were now well in the lead – and it was all their own fault.

Later that morning, all the Energy Zoners were standing together by the sports pitch next to the boating pond at Camp Sunshine. Becky had explained that morning that the day's challenge was to build a raft from various materials, including bits of plastic sheeting and wood.

Each team had the same equipment and Dom and Joe had given a demonstration of how to build a raft to all the Energy Zoners. The idea was that each of the teams had to remember what they had been shown and the challenge was to get two of their team on board the raft and successfully paddle it across the pond to the jetty on the other side.

"It didn't look that difficult when Dom and Joe did it," Flo said, trying to sound helpful.

"What did they do with these things?" Hannah held up some large pieces of plastic sheeting.

"They put them under the wood to water-proof it, didn't they?" Charly said.

"Yeah, one of the sheets," said Zoe. "Dom said we could use the other one as a sail if we wanted."

But every time the Glitter Girls tried to tie things together, something seemed to fall off.

"This is hopeless!" said Charly, angrily throw-ing a piece of wood down on to the grass.

"We might as well give up now," agreed Flo. "Look – the other teams are way ahead of us."

"I can't believe you lot!" Hannah said. "We're the Glitter Girls! We never give up!"

"She's right!" said Meg. "If we give up now the boys will really have something to gloat about!"

The Glitter Girls looked at each other and sighed.

"So?" Meg asked her friends. "Are we going to do this or not?"

"Yes," they all said determinedly.

By the time all the teams had finished, the Glitter Girls' raft certainly didn't look the prettiest but it did look like a raft – of sorts. Dom, Becky, Danny and Joe came round and inspected the four different rafts.

"Well, it's not the best presentation," Becky said when she got to the Glitter Girls. "But you have managed to include a sail. I'll give you three out of a possible five. We'll see how it floats in a minute."

The Animal Lovers got five for their raft

because it looked really good. And the Wild Wons and the Beastie Boyz got four each.

"So who's going to go on the raft?" Meg asked, as all four teams carried their rafts down to the water's edge.

"I will," said Zoe. "I'm a good swimmer so if we sink I'll be OK."

"Me too," said Hannah.

"OK," Meg, Flo and Charly agreed.

"Good luck," said Charly, giving her friends a hug.

The Glitter Girls were the first to go.

Zoe and Hannah put on their life jackets and climbed aboard. Then Meg, Flo and Charly gently pushed the raft from the shore. Using flat pieces of wood as paddles, the Glitter Girls' raft floated slowly to the other side.

"Yes!" Charly, Meg and Flo said with satisfaction as Joe helped their friends ashore.

The Animal Lovers' raft also made it across to the other side with ease but the Wild Wons got into trouble because their raft started to sink halfway across! Danny and Becky had to row across in a boat to rescue them.

The Beastie Boyz were last to go and were very confident. Nick and Jack pushed off the raft from the side and attempted to jump on board. But the unsteady motion caused by the two boys proved a bit of a disaster – Nick didn't get on at all and Jack only just managed to get on board. The raft got to the other side but with only one sailor.

In the meantime, everyone had run round to the other side of the pond where Becky and Dom were busy talking with Danny and Joe.

"So, who's won?" Senami asked.

"OK," said Joe. "Five each to the girls' teams because both their rafts got safely across the pond. Only two to the Beastie Boyz though because they only managed to get one person on the raft. No points to the Wild Wons because their raft sank."

All the boys groaned. But all the girls cheered.

"We beat them!" said Charly, jumping up and down with satisfaction.

"Yes!" her best friends replied.

"Huh!" said Jack, coming up to his sister. "But you're still not in the lead, are you? After all, you lost two points this morning!"

"That means we're on 44!" said Meg to her friends.

"The same as the Beasties!" sighed Hannah.

Now it was the Animal Lovers who were in the lead!

Chapter 9

"How are we going to catch up on this challenge?" Hannah wondered at breakfast the next morning.

"It's difficult to know unless we can find out what the next challenges are," Meg sighed.

"I know," said Flo. "It wouldn't be so bad if those boys weren't so smug all the time about beating us."

"If they weren't it wouldn't matter so much if we didn't win the challenge, would it?" Zoe said.

"Yeah, I mean, everything else here at Camp Sunshine is great," Hannah agreed.

It was true. Every afternoon when the day's challenge was complete, the Glitter Girls were able to swim, play games, go boating or just chill out in their cabin. They loved Camp Sunshine and were really pleased that they'd been able to come.

"I reckon we should just do our best to ignore those stupid boys," she suggested. "I mean, of course we should do our best in the challenges – but let's not let the boys spoil things for us."

"Meg's right," agreed Zoe.

"Yes," said Charly. "If we win, we win. Let's just have a laugh!"

"Go Glitter!" her friends agreed.

After breakfast, Becky announced that the day's challenge involved a trip to a local animal sanctuary. "You're going to do a quiz," Becky explained. "So grab your seats on the coach and we'll be off in half an hour!"

Arriving at the animal sanctuary, the Glitter Girls were reminded of the donkey sanctuary they visited at home. The one here was like a little farm with lots of different kinds of cute animals to see – as well as some donkeys.

Dom gave each team a list of questions and told them that they would find the answers by making their way around the place. Some of the questions were quite difficult, and involved having to find out about where the animals came from or identify the kind of prints their hooves left in mud.

There were 20 questions in all and Danny told them that if they got them all correct the total score would be ten points.

"Some of these are easy peasy!" exclaimed Meg when she first saw the list.

"Well, let's hope that we get them all right!" smiled Charly. "Come on – the first one is about the heavy horses. Apparently there's one called Harry and he's stabled over there."

"Where?" asked Flo and then she spotted that Zoe had already made her way over to Harry.

She laughed. "Surprise surprise! Zoe's found him!"

"Come on – let's get on with the questions," said Hannah and linked her arm into Meg's as they walked over to Zoe.

★ ♥ ★ ♥ ★ ♥ ★

The Glitter Girls made their way around the sanctuary, cooing at the animals that they saw. There were some rescued owls, which were so cute, lots of rabbits and even some llamas! One of them spat at Jack which the Glitter Girls found very amusing! Finally, it was time for lunch.

"If I could have everyone's attention? Please?" Danny said, his arm held in the air. In his hand he had the quiz papers.

The Energy Zoners were busy eating and chattering away about all the things they had seen that morning.

"I think they've worked out the scores!" Hannah whispered to the others.

"I wonder if we did as well as we think we did?" said Charly.

"Right," Danny continued. "Scores for today's challenge are: in joint first place the Wild Wons and the Glitter Girls with ten points each! Well done on getting full marks, you guys. The Animal Lovers and the Beastie Boyz both got eight points."

"No way!" protested Jack. "We got them all right!"

"You couldn't have," said Meg. "If you had you'd have got ten points."

"But we knew all the answers," moaned Will.

"Sorry, boys," Joe said. "The questions were set by the guys who run this place and we were really careful when we marked things. Looks like you got some things wrong today."

"So, what are the overall scores?" Ria wanted to know. "Are we still in the lead?" The Animal

Lovers were looking very pleased with themselves.

"Sorry, girls," Danny smiled sympathetically. "The Glitter Girls are back in the lead with 54 points. The Animal Lovers have 53 and the Beastie Boyz are close behind with 52. Bringing up the rear are the Wild Wons with 49."

"Go Glitter!" the five best friends couldn't help shouting.

"Excuse me," said Zoe, stifling a yawn.

The Glitter Girls were back in their cabin getting ready for bed after a busy afternoon and evening.

"I think you spent too much time on the trampoline!" laughed Meg, who was pretty exhausted herself from the tennis game they'd played.

"That chess game is great," said Hannah. The girls had had a great time playing with the giant chessboard and pieces – it was just like the one in Harry Potter! "I wish we had one like that at the Rec back home."

"What was that?" Charly asked, as she brushed her hair.

"What?" said Zoe.

"That noise!" said Charly. "There was a noise outside the window."

"I didn't hear anything," Meg said.

"Here, let me look." Hannah pulled back the edge of the curtain – just in time to see someone's head bob down below the window ledge. She let go of the curtain quickly and turned back to her friends. "Shh! It's a boy!"

"Who?" her friends asked.

"My brother?" Meg whispered.

"I don't know if it's him but one of the Beasties is outside the window," explained Hannah.

"I suppose he's trying to spook us like he did at the sleepover that time," Charly whispered.

"Well let's spook him instead!" said Meg.

"Quick, everyone – grab your torch and come and stand by the window."

The girls leapt out of bed and stood beside Hannah with their torches.

"What are we going to do?" whispered Zoe.

"Watch," Meg replied. "Charly, can you turn off the lights? When I say 'GG' everyone switch on your torch and scream as loudly as you can."

The Glitter Girls silently nodded. Meg peeped through a tiny slit in the middle of the curtains. In the silence, they could hear whispering outside. Meg saw someone move. They started to moan.

"GG!" she whispered.

The Glitter Girls switched on their torches and screamed with all their might as Meg pulled back the curtains.

"Aaarrgh!" came a frightened scream from outside, and the Glitter Girls ran to the door in time to see a very scared Jack and Nick run back to the boys' cabin. They all burst out laughing.

"Got them!" Meg managed to splutter through her laughter.

"Go Glitter!"

Chapter 10

"What day is it today?" Charly asked, as the Glitter Girls sat in the dining room eating their breakfast and writing postcards.

"Umm – it must be Thursday," said Zoe.

"Already?" Flo was amazed.

"It's incredible, isn't it?" said Hannah.

"The week has just whizzed by," agreed Meg. "There's so much to do here. Hey, look – Joe's coming over."

"Morning, everyone," Joe said. "I suppose you all want to know what challenge we've set for you today."

"Yes!" came the enthusiastic reply.

Joe laughed. "Well – it's a treasure hunt!"

"Where do we do that?" Fizz asked.

"Here at Camp Sunshine." Joe explained.

"What's the treasure?" Jack wanted to know.

"Pieces of jigsaw," Danny said.

"What?" asked Jack, pulling a face. "Some treasure!"

"How do we know where to find it?" Zoe asked.

"We've got some clues for you!" Dom said, handing round a sheet of paper to each group. "The clues should lead you to the jigsaw pieces and then when you've got them all you'll have the final clue that will lead you to the treasure."

"But what if another team gets to the jigsaw pieces first?" said Nick. "That wouldn't be fair!"

There were murmurs of agreement from the others.

"Don't worry," Danny explained. We've thought of that. Each team has different clues. So there are five pieces of each puzzle for your team to collect – and if you are tempted to pinch another team's clue, don't! Because it won't fit into your jigsaw!"

"Ready?" Joe asked. "Then take a look at your team's clues and get treasure hunting!"

★ ♥ ★ ♥ ★ ♥ ★

It didn't take the Glitter Girls long to find the first two pieces of their jigsaw. Like all the other teams, the first one was in their own cabin. For the Glitter Girls, the second was in the girls' shower room. But the third clue had the girls puzzled.

"All it says is: 'up high is where to find it. Puzzled? Just a little bit!' It doesn't narrow it down!" Hannah despaired.

"Up high, but where?" sighed Charly.

"Who knows," said Zoe, slumping down on the grass outside the shower block.

"Here," said Flo. "Let me see those clues."

Hannah handed them to her to read.

"Well the fourth clue must be somewhere near the boating pond because it says: 'don't sink or swim but keep afloat to find your way towards some groats'," said Flo.

"What's a groat?" asked Zoe, puzzled.

"I think it's an old word for money or some-thing – it must mean the treasure," Meg said.

"Why don't we go straight to the pond then?" Hannah suggested.

"But we can't," said Zoe. "We haven't worked out this clue yet."

"There's nothing in the instructions to say that we have to do the clues in order, is there?" Charly pointed out.

"Let's go then!" said Meg.

The Glitter Girls ran towards the boating pond. After a little searching, they found the jigsaw piece inside one of the boats that was still tied up to the jetty.

"I can't see any of the other teams," said Zoe as she put the piece in her rucksack.

"No," agreed Flo.

The Glitter Girls looked round them as they

listened to Meg reading out the fifth clue: " 'Where you eat, but don't eat me, or the last you will not see!' " said Meg.

"The cafeteria!" the others all said at once.

"Come on," Hannah yelled and off they all ran.

Sure enough, the Glitter Girls found another piece of puzzle waiting for them in the cafeteria, near to the trays.

"So we've just got the third clue left," said Zoe. She read it out again. "But what does it mean?" she moaned.

"I still have no idea where we're meant to go – 'up high'. . ." puzzled Charly.

"Neither do I," sighed Flo.

"It's nearly twelve o'clock," Charly said worriedly. "Only another half hour until lunch. We're running out of time!"

"Well," said Meg. "Why don't we walk round the camp and see if we get any ideas?"

"Good thinking," said Hannah.

★ ♥ ★ ♥ ★ ♥ ★

For fifteen minutes the Glitter Girls wandered around the camp aimlessly, still as puzzled as ever about the clue. As they walked they looked up to see if they could get any ideas.

"This is so irritating!" Zoe moaned.

"'Up high'. 'Up high' – where can it be?" wondered Charly.

Just then, they approached the rope walk.

"Hey!" Hannah exclaimed. "The rope walk – that's up high, isn't it!"

"Yes!" exclaimed Meg. She looked at her watch. "Come on – we've only got fifteen minutes to go. We've got to find the clue and we've still got to make it back to the cafeteria in time – way over on the other side of the camp!"

★ ♥ ★ ♥ ★ ♥ ★

"So what kept you, girls?" Jack sniggered as the Glitter Girls raced back into the cafeteria, breathless from running. They had found the last piece of their puzzle and put it together with the others. Then they read the final clue which was actually just a message from Becky and Dom telling them to get back to the common room, fast!

Now that they were there, a quick glance around the room proved to them that they were indeed the last team to make it back.

"Are we on time?" Flo pleaded with Becky.

"Just," she smiled. "You only had one minute to go. We were getting worried about you."

"Phew!" sighed Hannah.

"Right – today's scores. . ." said Joe.

The room fell silent. With only today's and tomorrow's challenges to count, everyone knew just how close they were to finding out if their team had won the Camp Sunshine challenge.

"Everyone gets five points for finding all their jigsaw," said Joe.

There was applause all round.

"But!" Joe continued. "We've got some adjust-ments to make due to the order that you finished in," he continued.

"The Wild Wons came back first so they get an extra two points – making their new total 56."

There was a reluctant round of applause from the other teams but the Wild Wons were clapping themselves enthusiastically.

"Animal Lovers you just add five to your score taking you to 58. . ."

Everyone clapped again.

"The Beastie Boyz get five and move up to 57. . ."

More clapping.

"But the Glitter Girls, I'm afraid you lose two points for coming back last. . ."

"Ha ha!" said Jack, smirking at his sister.

"That's enough, Jack," Joe cautioned. "So that makes the Glitter Girls' total 57."

"I can't bear it," sighed Meg. "That means that we're back on the same score as the Beastie Boyz!"

Chapter 11

The Glitter Girls commiserated with each other by having a midnight feast that night . . . and were very tired when they were woken for breakfast the next morning.

Still, it was a beautiful sunny day and the warmth of the sun soon made them wake up and look forward to whatever challenge Becky, Dom, Danny and Joe had planned for them. Their last challenge at Camp Sunshine.

"Today we're heading for the beach." Becky smiled.

"Yes!" said all the Energy Zoners.

"Your challenge," Becky continued, "is to build the biggest and most beautiful sandcastle!"

"Hooray!" Jack and the other boys cheered.

"The cleverer your design the more points you will score," Danny said.

"And you'll have until midday to complete your masterpieces," Joe added.

"And then we'll have a picnic lunch, and hopefully some free time. Although we have to watch the tide – the tide timetable says it will start to come in later this morning."

"So," Dom said. "Go get your beach stuff and then meet us back at the coach in twenty minutes."

★ ♥ ★ ♥ ★ ♥ ★

The beach they were taken to was really lovely. It was mostly sand with very little shingle, and white cliffs surrounded it. There was also a sort of cave area at the back of the beach. On the coach, Dom had warned them all not to stray when they were on the beach.

"There's a cliff path that runs very close to the edge and goes up quite high," he had said.

"And no mucking about on the rocks because when the tide comes in they get submerged under the water – and we don't want anyone getting stuck! When the tide comes in it's fast and strong, and there's a dangerous current. It's not something even the best swimmers can handle. OK?"

Now they were actually on the beach, the Glitter Girls could see exactly what Dom had meant.

"We don't want to go too near the water over there," Zoe warned, pointing towards the rocks. "Otherwise we could run the risk of losing our sandcastle to the sea before we've finished."

"This looks like a good spot, here," suggested Flo, putting her towel down.

So the Glitter Girls picked their patch on the sand and were pleased to see that Jack and the Beastie Boyz had chosen a spot that was quite some way from them.

"Right," said Meg. "We need a plan."

"OK," the others agreed.

"I've been thinking about the design. . ." offered Flo.

"Great," said Meg.

The other girls nodded.

"Hannah, why don't you and I go and get the spades and stuff from Dom?" Charly suggested.

Hannah nodded and they wandered over to Dom.

"Shall we start collecting some pebbles to use as decorations, Zoe?" Meg asked.

"Sure," Zoe agreed.

The Glitter Girls got to work. Flo came up with a great design for the castle that included three different tiers. The pebbles were going to be used as markers for the arrow slits in the castle walls. There was also a plan for a moat – Flo had even come up with a plan to see if they could find a piece of wood that had been swept ashore to use for a moving drawbridge!

Every now and then, Dom, Becky, Danny and Joe came round to all of the teams to see how they were doing.

"Make sure you keep your hats on and top up your sunscreen," Danny warned. "It's pretty hot today."

To cool themselves off, the Glitter Girls took it in turns to take a break from their hard work and paddled in the sea. Meg and Zoe took the chance to see what the other teams were up to while they were paddling – the Glitter Girls had been so busy that they hadn't had a chance to look at their opponents until then. Further up the beach, the Wild Wons and the Animal Lovers were hard at work on their castles. But the Beastie Boyz seemed to be concentrating their efforts on flicking sand at each other.

"Typical," Meg thought as she saw Jack and Nick chasing each other to the rocks.

"You boys come away from there!" Danny yelled, starting after them.

But Jack and Nick were so busy acting the fool that they didn't seem to hear him.

Just then there was a piercing scream close to Meg and Zoe.

"Owwww! Help!"

Chapter 12

Suddenly the quiet beach was transformed into a commotion with people scrambling to find out what was going on and who was yelling.

Ria had fallen down amongst the shingle. As soon as he had heard her scream, Danny left his pursuit of the boys and began running back towards Ria.

"Quick!" Meg called to her friends. "Ria needs help!"

"It hurts!" Ria cried. By the time the Glitter Girls got to her, Ria's ankle was already red and swollen. Soon everyone was crowding round.

"We need to get you back to the bus," Becky said. "Danny! Joe! Can you help, please?"

"OK!" Danny said. "Come on, you lot – the sandcastles can wait while we sort out Ria."

"But we haven't finished yet!" protested some of the Wild Wons.

"Well, we can't leave you down here on the beach alone. Sorry, guys, you'll have to leave the sandcastles – everyone get their things together and follow us back up to the car park," Joe said.

"Poor Ria," said Charly. "She's really in pain."

Ria was crying her eyes out and her face was screwed up in agony.

"I think I need to get her to A and E," Dom said. "We should get this ankle X-rayed." He and Becky had begun to get Ria to her feet and help her limp towards the car park.

"I'll get everyone back on the bus," Danny said. "Let me just count heads. . ."

"Hey, look!" Meg nudged her friends.

Over by the far end of the beach, Jack, Nick and the other Beastie Boyz were oblivious to the drama that was unfolding and were still larking about. Only now they had waded out to the rocks and climbed up out of the water. They saw the Glitter Girls looking at them and waved and made monkey actions.

The Glitter Girls laughed – trust them to dare to go on the rocks and lark about. But suddenly Danny spotted them.

"Oh no! What are those idiots doing?" he shouted, and began running towards the far end of the beach. "I thought I told you to come back! Come back right now, you twits! Can't you see the tide's coming in? You'll get cut off! Come back right this minute!" Danny shouted, looking really angry. But the boys were too far away to hear. The Glitter Girls and Joe followed Danny, running as fast as they could after him. They were all out of breath when they reached the stretch of water that separated the rocks from the beach.

'Come back!" shouted Danny again.

Only they couldn't. In the short time that the Beasties had been on the rocks, the tide had been coming in quickly, just as they had been warned – and now the water was high up against the rocks, the strong current making it swirl in all directions. It had become much deeper too – deeper than any water the boys had ever swum in before.

"Danny!" cried Meg, nervous for her brother. "They can't get back! The Beasties are in trouble – I think they've been cut off by the tide!"

★ ♥ ★ ♥ ★ ♥ ★

"Help!" Jack called, looking gingerly at the turbulent water that surrounded the rocks.

"Please! We're stuck!" yelled Fizz.

The look on the boys' faces had changed from laughter to panic.

"What should we do?" Charly said anxiously.

"We need to get help," said Danny. "The tide's

still coming in and the water is only going to get deeper."

"And we need to get Ria to hospital too!" exclaimed Flo, looking back towards the car park where the others were waiting with Becky by the coach.

"But we can't leave the boys here on their own!" said Zoe, panic in her voice.

"Hannah – rush to the coach and tell Becky what's happened," said Danny. "She can use her phone to call the coastguard while they are on their way to the hospital."

"But the water's getting deeper by the minute," Meg said worriedly. "We can't wait that long!"

"Don't worry, Meg. They'll be all right," Joe said, not sounding very convinced. "We've just got to get help and we haven't a moment to lose."

"I'm off!" said Hannah, heading back towards the car park.

By now the Beastie Boyz were looking very worried indeed. The rocks were disappearing rapidly under the rising water. They were screaming out to the others, begging for help.

"I'm sure I remember seeing a lifebelt somewhere along the cliff path. I'll go and get it," said Joe, racing off.

"We can't stand here doing nothing!" said Charly.

"There's only one lifebelt," Meg cried. "They can't all wait to use that!"

"OK, everyone get their jackets and towels and things. If we tie them all together, maybe we can make a lifeline. . ." said Danny.

"Quick, everyone! Come on – we haven't got a moment to lose!" said Charly.

Everyone rushed back with their stuff and they all helped Danny tie towels, jackets and beach wraps together to make a rope. By the time they'd finished, Joe had returned, breathless, from the cliff path.

"Here," said Joe, handing Danny the lifebelt.

"Thanks," said Danny, grabbing the belt and rushing towards the sea. "Some of you hold on to the rope with Joe as ballast! The rest of you keep adding to that lifeline!"

Danny ran into the water until it was almost up to his shoulders while Charly, Flo, Zoe and Meg and the others held tight to the rope.

"Please say he's going to be all right!" Meg cried.

"It's OK, Meg," Charly said, trying to comfort her. "Danny'll help them."

With all his might, Danny threw the lifebelt towards the rocks. The Beastie Boyz leant out trying to grab it, but they missed. Jack was so anxious to catch it he leant too far forward and lost his grip! He slid towards the water and the Glitter Girls gasped in horror. Just in time, Nick and Fizz had managed to grab hold of his T-shirt and pull him back.

Frantically, Danny pulled the lifebelt back towards him, fighting against the strength of the water. It seemed incredible that on such a quiet sunny day, the sea could be so dangerous.

With the second throw, Jack somehow managed to hook the lifebelt. He looked terrified.

"Climb into it!" Danny yelled.

At the same time that Jack jumped into the sea with the belt, Joe threw himself into the sea from the beach, the lifeline of clothes and towels tied securely round his own waist.

"Swim, Jack!" Meg yelled from the beach. "Please swim!"

But, like the others, Meg could see that even with the lifebelt on, Jack was struggling and being buffeted by the waves. Even Joe was having to fight to move forward in the water as the current was so strong.

"Hold on to it tight!" yelled Joe to Jack as he

waded deeper towards the rocks in the hope of rescuing more of the Beastie Boyz.

"Hey, listen!" said Charly.

"What?" asked Meg, anxiously.

But then she heard it herself. In the distance there was the noise of an engine humming. And then they saw it – a lifeboat! The coast-guard had sent a lifeboat to rescue the Beasties!

The large red speedboat pulled up next to the rocks and remained steady against the powerful current. One of the lifeboatmen managed to get close enough to leap on to the rocks and hand Nick a life jacket. It wasn't long before all the boys were kitted out. The man then helped them one by one to swim from the rocks to the safety of the lifeboat. Joe had waded back out of the water because the Glitter Girls' lifeline was no longer needed – the coastguards had proper lifebelts to help the boys swim to safety.

Meg was nearly crying with relief as she saw

Jack clamber aboard the powerful boat. By the time all the boys had swum across he looked much calmer and seemed to be chatting to one of the coastguards about the speedboat. "Typical!" said Meg to the other Glitter Girls, but she was too relieved to do anything but laugh.

"Look," said Zoe, pointing to where the rocks had been. "The tide's come in so much that the rocks are now under the water!"

"They were so lucky the lifeboat turned up when it did," said Flo, hugging Meg.

Danny and Joe were listening as the lifeboatmen yelled across to them, telling them where they'd be taking the boys. Danny then turned to the Glitter Girls and said, "That's enough excitement for one day, I think! Are you girls all OK?"

The girls mumbled something in reply, still dazed by what had just happened.

"Come on," said Joe wearily, "Let's all head back to the car park and pick up the boys."

Chapter 13

A while later, the shocked members of the Energy Zone met up again, at the hospital. Dom and Joe were sitting outside on a patch of grass with most of the Energy Zoners. Becky was inside with Ria while her ankle was being treated. Danny was with the Beasties who were being treated for shock. Everyone had been reunited with the Beasties at the hospital after the lifeboatmen had taken them back to a waiting ambulance at the harbour.

Exhausted from the near-disastrous day, the group sat quietly and were relieved when Becky finally said they were almost ready to head back to camp.

"Well – I reckon that today's challenge was

one that none of us will ever forget!" said Danny, looking sternly around the common room after they had disembarked from the coach.

"And not one that we would want to repeat!" added Dom, wearily.

Jack and the other Beastie Boyz looked embarrassed. Ria was sitting with her friends, nursing her bandaged ankle. It turned out that she had sprained it really badly, but luckily it wasn't broken.

"That was a close thing back there!" Joe said.

"Sorry," said Nick.

"Sorry," said the other Beasties.

"I'm really glad you're safe," Meg whispered, touching her brother's arm. She was sitting on a bench just behind Jack and for the first time that holiday she suddenly felt really pleased he was there.

"Quite frankly," Danny said to the Beasties, "I think you should thank your friends here. If it hadn't been for their quick work this afternoon you might not be here now!"

The Beasties hung their heads in embarrassment.

After a few moments of silence, Jack spoke again. "Danny?"

"Yes, mate?"

"Thanks, and that. . . Actually, I was just wondering," Jack said, scratching his head. "Which team won the sandcastle competition today?"

There was a groan of disbelief from Danny, Becky, Joe, Dom and the other Energy Zoners.

"You have to be joking!" spluttered Meg. "After everything that happened today! And you are worried about your sandcastle?"

"I just wanted to know if we'd won!" Jack protested.

"Get a life, Jack!" said Charly.

"Well?" whined Nick. "Someone has to win the challenge!"

The cafeteria was now a hubbub of noise.

"Surprisingly," Danny said sarcastically, "we did not get the opportunity to judge the sand-castles today. . ."

"So does that mean yesterday's scores still stand?" Ria asked, keen to know if despite her calamitous day, the Animal Lovers had won the Camp Sunshine challenge.

"Yes. . ." said Dom. "At the moment."

"What?" Will whined. "But that's not fair!"

"I think we need to think about it," Joe said, looking at the other leaders.

"Yes," agreed Danny.

"And, in the meantime, we need to tell you about what we've got planned for your last day at Camp Sunshine," explained Becky.

The Glitter Girls looked at each other. It seemed impossible that their week's holiday was almost over already.

"You're free to spend the rest of today and tomorrow morning doing whatever activities you like here at Camp Sunshine," Becky explained.

"Only you might want to practise," said Danny.

"Practise for what?" Zoe asked.

"Karaoke," said Joe, grinning at the surprised Energy Zoners. "We're having a big barbecue party to celebrate our last night here tomorrow and we thought you lot could provide the entertainment."

"Karaoke!" Charly grinned excitedly.

"Karaoke!" Becky confirmed.

"Go Glitter!" Charly, Meg, Zoe, Flo and Hannah all said at once.

Chapter 14

Back in their cabin, the Glitter Girls were trying to decide what they were going to do for the karaoke competition.

"We could do the Sugababes' latest hit!" suggested Charly, pushing her pink glasses back up on her nose.

"Or how about Atomic Kitten?" wondered Flo.

"Or S Club Juniors?" said Hannah, who loved all their great dance routines.

"We can't do one of their songs because we haven't got any boys in our team," Zoe pointed out.

"Well we could team up with Jack and Nick!" said Charly, laughing wickedly.

"You have to be kidding!" said Meg. "I know I'm pleased he's OK – but no *way*!"

The Glitter Girls laughed.

"The thing is though," said Hannah. "We haven't got much in the way of costumes or anything with us, have we?"

"True. . ." said Meg thoughtfully.

"But I've got some make-up with me," Flo said.

"And I brought some hair-braiding stuff," explained Zoe. "I thought we'd have plenty of time to do it earlier this week – I hadn't realized that we'd be so busy!"

"Great," said Charly. "But what about clothes?"

"We can just wear our Glitter Girl stuff," Hannah suggested, "and maybe just add things like . . . more glitter!"

"Yeah, that'll be fine," Meg confirmed. "But what are we going to sing?"

"How about a song by that band that won the Pop Rivals competition?" suggested Flo. "You know – Girls Aloud!"

"Yes!" said Zoe. "They're an all-girl band."

"And there are five of them!" added Hannah.

"We could call ourselves Glitter Girls Aloud!" grinned Charly.

"Perfect!" said Meg.

"Go Glitter!" her friends confirmed.

Fortunately, Charly had Girls Aloud's latest hit on a compilation CD that she had brought with her to Camp Sunshine. So the Glitter Girls spent a happy time that afternoon learning all the words to the song. While they were doing that, Hannah concentrated on working out some dance steps.

"Come on – see if you can copy me," Hannah urged when she had the routine in her own head.

"But there isn't enough space here!" protested Charly.

She was right – with the three sets of bunk

beds, there wasn't a lot of floor space.

"Well, let's practise outside then," suggested Zoe.

"But everyone else will see us!" Flo pointed out.

"I know!" said Meg, standing up. "Let's take Charly's Discman with us and we can rehearse on the recreation ground."

"Go Glitter!"

The Glitter Girls even did some more rehearsing after supper and really got in to the swing of it. They found themselves humming the tune as they changed for bed.

They climbed under their duvets and talked about all the adventures they had had that week.

"You know, we could ask Danny if he could organize another orienteering thing for us when we are back home," Meg suggested. "It was so much fun."

"I thought the animal sanctuary was the best," said Zoe, which didn't surprise her friends much.

"The animals were cute, weren't they?" said Charly.

"I liked all of it," said Flo. "Except maybe when the boys got stranded. . ."

"Yes," said Hannah. "That was scary, wasn't it?"

"My mum will go nuts when she finds out what Jack and Nick did," said Meg. She snuggled down under her duvet, grateful that everything had turned out all right in the end.

"Even so," sighed Hannah. "It's been a good week, hasn't it?"

"Excellent," agreed Charly.

"Despite not beating the Beastie Boyz in the challenge," said Flo, yawning. "It's been one of the best."

The Glitter Girls were so tired after their busy

day, that even they couldn't talk any more.

★ ♥ ★ ♥ ★ ♥ ★

After breakfast the next morning, the Glitter Girls had another rehearsal, this time in the girls' shower block, so that they could see themselves in the mirrors.

"I think we just need to perfect the ending," Hannah said, wanting to make sure that the Glitter Girls got everything just right.

"Then I think we could give it a break for a bit," said Meg. "After all – we can't perfect on perfect can we?"

"But what shall we do for the rest of the day?" wondered Zoe.

"We've got our make-up and stuff to do," said Flo.

"We can do that later," suggested Charly.

"Well, let's go swimming," said Meg. "After all, we won't get a chance to swim in such a great pool after today, will we?"

"As long as we can go on the trampolines too," agreed Hannah.

"Go Glitter!"

Chapter 15

"You look fantastic!" said Becky, greeting the Glitter Girls as they arrived at the common room later that evening.

"Thanks!" said Meg. "When do we get to do the karaoke?"

"We thought we could do it before everyone eats," said Danny. "That way the food can be cooking while we enjoy all your acts!"

"Hey, look at Ria!" said Hannah.

"Cool!" exclaimed Flo.

Ria had decorated the bandage on her foot with ribbons and badges and was sitting on a chair looking a lot happier than she had yesterday.

"Hi Ria," Zoe waved. "Like your foot decorations!"

"Thanks." Ria grinned. "Heard you were doing Girls Aloud tonight."

"That's right," said Charly. "With a Glitter Girl twist!"

"What about the Animal Lovers?" Meg asked.

"We're doing an Atomic Kitten number," Ria smiled. "And I've heard the Beastie Boyz are going to be Blue."

"Hey, look, there they are!" Zoe pointed to the boys, who were coming across the lawn towards the party.

The Glitter Girls had to admit that in their jeans and T-shirts with their hair all spiked up with wax, Jack, Nick and the other Beasties did look pretty cool. As for the Wild Wons, they had chosen to cover a Westlife number – only they called themselves Wildlife!

"Right, now that everyone's here. . ." Danny began, "let the party begin! Come on – let's see everyone dancing. Warm yourselves up for the karaoke."

"When are we going to eat?" Jack wanted to know.

"Always thinking of food, aren't you?" Meg said, exasperated.

"Don't worry about it, Jack," Danny laughed. "We're having the barbecue after the karaoke. Meantime, let's dance."

He flicked a switch near to the music system and not only did the disco music start but the lights got going too! There was a huge glitter-ball hanging from the ceiling and the hall had been decorated especially. There were lots of other groups dancing too; obviously it was everyone's last night at Camp Sunshine.

"Hurray!" the Energy Zoners yelled as the last night party got going.

★ ♥ ★ ♥ ★ ♥ ★

Everyone was having a great time and it was even better when the karaoke began.

"Good luck, everyone," Hannah said to her

friends when it was their turn. She counted them in. "Five, six, seven, eight. . ."

The Glitter Girls sang their hearts out. And they loved every minute of it. It seemed like no time at all before their routine came to an end though.

"Way to go, girls!" Joe called and led the audience in the applause.

"Who's next?" Danny asked, looking at his list. "The Beastie Boyz doing Blue!"

There was more applause as Meg's brother and his friends stepped out in front of everyone and took up their positions, just like the real Blue line-up. Everyone was impressed. The Beasties really put on a performance!

"We did really well, I think," Meg said to her friends as the music ended.

"Yeah," grinned Hannah.

"A real Glitter Girl special," said Charly.

"The boys were really good too!" said Flo.

And so were the Animal Lovers, who looked

fantastic in their outfits and the Wildlife Wild Wons, who made everyone laugh with their pouting!

"Thank goodness we didn't have to judge this," said Danny at the end. "Well done, everyone – you were all brilliant!"

"The challenge!" Meg said. "You haven't told us who won the challenge!"

"Hey, that's right!" said Jack. "Have you made a decision yet?"

"Well," said Becky, looking at Danny and Joe. "We decided that we couldn't do anything about the sandcastle challenge. . ."

"But ours was the best!" protested Jack.

"Hardly!" said Charly.

"Yes!" said Ria. "Until you lot spoilt everything my team was doing pretty well!"

"We spoilt it!" spluttered Nick. "What about you falling over?"

"That's enough, you lot!" said Joe. "Do you want to know what we've decided, or what?"

"Yes!" everyone said.

The Glitter Girls looked at each other. They knew that if the scores still stood at Thursday night's tally, then the Animal Lovers had beaten them with 58 points. And the Glitter Girls' score was going to be one behind them at 57. The same as the Beastie Boyz – but at least it meant that they wouldn't have a score that was lower than them. The poor Wild Wons were stuck on 56.

"So," Danny carried on. "The winning team is. . ."

Joe played a drum role on the music system.

". . . the Animal Lovers!"

The Glitter Girls cheered and clapped like everyone else. Of course they were disappointed that they didn't win, but the Animal Lovers had won fairly.

"Hey, thanks!" the Animal Lovers said, going up to collect some certificates that Becky had made for them.

"And we've got these for you too," said Danny, handing over a huge tin of sweets.

"Never mind," Meg said, hugging Charly who was standing next to her.

"Yes," said Zoe. "Ria deserves it after hurting her foot like that."

Ria and the other Animal Lovers were chatting to each other and looking at their prize. Suddenly, Ria hobbled over to Becky and after a brief conversation with her, the music was turned down again and Ria spoke to everyone.

"We want to share the sweets with everyone," Ria said, holding the tin out in front of her. "After all, if I hadn't fallen over and hurt my foot you wouldn't have needed to abandon the challenge in the first place."

"And the Beastie Boyz wouldn't have gone on to cause so much trouble!" Meg said.

Everyone laughed.

"So, who wants a sweet?" Ria asked.

"Me!" yelled all the Energy Zoners, crowding round Ria.

"Thanks, Ria," Flo said, taking a chocolate cream.

"No problem," said Ria.

"Come on, everyone," Danny yelled. "Barbecue time!"

And the Camp Sunshine party carried on till late into the night.

★ ♥ ★ ♥ ★ ♥ ★

On Sunday morning, the Energy Zoners boarded their coach and said farewell to Becky and Dom.

"We've had a really brilliant time!" Charly said. "Thanks, Becky. Thanks, Dom."

"And I've had a great time too!" said Dom. "Come back next year!"

"Come on – we've got to get going," Danny said. "Otherwise your parents will be wondering what I've done with you all!"

Slowly, the coach pulled out of Camp Sunshine and the Energy Zoners waved to Becky and Dom until they couldn't see them any more.

"That was the best adventure I think we've ever had!" said Charly, slumping back into her seat at the back of the coach.

"Agreed," said Flo.

"I loved it!" sighed Zoe.

"Me too. . ." said Hannah, flicking her hair behind her ears. "Do you think it was the best, Meg?"

"Well . . . maybe," said Meg, smiling.

"What do you mean only 'maybe'?" Charly wanted to know.

"I agree it was the best adventure we've had this summer holiday," Meg grinned.

"But the summer holidays only started a week ago!" Flo said.

"Exactly," said Meg. "And we've got another five weeks to have even more fun!"

"Go Glitter!" her best friends confirmed!

Photo Fame

There was a big platform at one end of the hall and the panel of judges was seated right in front of it. Suddenly the enormous room fell silent as one of them stood up.

"Hello, everyone! I'm Matt and I'm the director of the two Ice Brite Glitter commercials that we are auditioning for today. I'd like to introduce you to Catriona who's from Ice Brite and who is here to help us to make sure we get the right smile today. . ." A lady with short dark hair stood up and smiled at everyone. Then

Matt started to speak again. "We've also got Vicki here with us, who is going to choreograph the commercial." Matt pointed out another girl next to him. "There's lots of you to see today so we'd better get on with things. OK – Miranda, let's have the first girls on stage please!"

The audition had begun.

For a large part of the audition, the Glitter Girls stood around with everyone else, not doing much at all. Eventually though, they got their chance to go up on the stage with a group of about twenty girls. The first thing they had to do was step forward, one at a time, to say their name and age again.

"Don't forget to smile!" Meg whispered as she went up with her friends.

But seconds later, their group was called off the stage again.

"What do you think they'll do next?" Flo

whispered to her friends once they were sitting down again.

"Decide who gets a chance to do their audition piece, I expect," said Charly.

"You mean some people will have come all the way here just to say their name and age?" Zoe said, amazed.

"That's right," said Meg. "Isn't it awful?"

After about another hour, Miranda came back and explained that only some of them were being called back for the next session.

"Listen carefully," Miranda said. "If we don't call your number, thank you for coming along today but, we're sorry, you aren't through to the next round. If we do call you though, please stay in your seat."

The friends grabbed each other's hands and held them tight. Were any of them going to be asked to go home already? Each of them was still hoping that one of the Glitter Girls was going to be chosen as the Ice Brite Smile.

At the same time they were dreading being one of the girls asked to leave. The butterflies in their tummies fluttered anxiously. But soon the girls' worries were over – all five of them had been called for the next round!

"Go Glitter!" they all said.

Miranda told them all to take their seats again and explained that they would be called up in turn to do their audition piece.

"Good job we decided to do a dance – seeing as one of the judges is a choreographer," Hannah whispered to her friends, and they all gave her a nervous smile of agreement.

★ ♥ ★ ♥ ★ ♥ ★

There was a lot more hanging around before the girls were called on stage. Or at least, when Zoe was called by Miranda.

When all five of them stood up at once, Miranda looked at them, puzzled. "Er, I only want one of you. . ." She looked down at her clipboard. "Which one of you is Zoe?"

"Oh – we're going to do our dance together," Hannah explained.

"Together?" the girl looked worried.

"Yes," said Zoe. "We're best friends, we do everything together."

"I see," she said. "I'll need to explain that to our panel of judges."

"They will let us do our piece together, won't they?" Meg asked. "We've rehearsed it that way so we have to!"

Miranda was still looking anxious. "Well it's not usual, I must say. I'll have to go and ask the judges if it's OK. Wait here a moment."

The Glitter Girls looked at each other.

"What will we do if they say no?" Zoe asked.

"We're best friends, aren't we?" Meg said, looking at her friends. "We do everything together – if they say no then we'll just have to leave now. Agreed?"

"Agreed!" the Glitter Girls said, crossing their fingers and hoping the judges would say yes.

It wasn't long before Miranda came back over to them.

"OK – they've said yes. Have you got any backing music?"

Zoe handed the tape to Miranda.

"You'll need to get over by the stage as soon as possible. Wait at the back of the queue."

"OK," nodded Flo.

"Phew!" said Meg. "Come on, let's get the wrapping off our props and go!"

The Glitter Girls, along with their toothbrush and toothpaste, joined the other girls by the stage.

One by one, the girls in front of them went up to perform their piece. Some of them sang, some danced, some recited poems. All of them were really talented.

"This is really scary!" whispered Flo. "Why are we doing this?"

"It'll be fine," said Hannah. But she didn't sound like she believed it.

"It's your turn now!" said Miranda, ushering them on to the stage. "Good luck!"

Meg, Flo, Hannah, Zoe and Charly looked at each other and gulped.

"Go Glitter!" they whispered.